Look to the Night Sky
An Introduction to Star Watching

From the beginning of time people have looked to the night sky for omens, for information, for the sheer wonder of it. And today we can continue to observe stars, planets, comets, and meteors, much as people have done for thousands of years.

This book explains how to look at the stars without equipment any more sophisticated or expensive than your own eyes, and how to understand what you are seeing. And, as you learn to recognize many things—constellations, the visible difference between planets and stars, the phases of the moon, and where to look for meteors—you will begin to grasp the awesome magnificence of our solar system and the universe.

AN OUTSTANDING SCIENCE TRADE BOOK,
National Science Teachers Association

Other Puffin Science Books by Seymour Simon are

LOOK
TO THE
NIGHT SKY

An Introduction to Star Watching

SEYMOUR SIMON

PUFFIN BOOKS

Penguin Books Ltd, Harmondsworth, Middlesex, England
Penguin Books, 625 Madison Avenue, New York, New York 10022, U.S.A.
Penguin Books Australia Ltd, Ringwood, Victoria, Australia
Penguin Books Canada Limited, 2801 John Street, Markham, Ontario, Canada L3R 1B4
Penguin Books (N.Z.) Ltd, 182–190 Wairau Road, Auckland 10, New Zealand

First published by The Viking Press 1977
Published in Puffin Books 1979

Library of Congress Cataloging in Publication Data
Simon, Seymour. Look to the night sky.
Bibliography: p.   Includes index.
Summary: Explains how to observe stars with the naked
eye and how to understand what is seen. Discusses
the difference between astronomy and astrology.
1. Astronomy—Observers' manuals—Juvenile literature.
[1. Astronomy—Observers' manuals] I. Title.
QB64.S55 1979   523   79-1329   ISBN 0-14-049185-6

Printed in the United States of America by
The Book Press, Brattleboro, Vermont
Set in Bodoni

Photo Credits: Lunar & Planetary Laboratory,
University of Arizona (copyright pending) : Pages 40, 41, 42
Hale Observatories: Pages 48, 53
The Kitt Peak National Observatory: Pages 70, 72, 73, 75, 76

For all my friends in the Junior Astronomy Club

CONTENTS

INTRODUCTION
TO THE NIGHT SKY

*G*o out of doors on a clear, moonless night. Pick a time at least one hour after sunset, when the last pale gleam of sunlight has faded from the sky. Look up at the sky. About how many stars do you see? Tens? Hundreds? Would you like to see many more? Try this.

Sit down or lean against something. Close your eyes and count slowly up to two hundred. Keep your eyes shut as you count. Now open your eyes and look at the stars. They seem to fill the sky. The bright stars look brighter and many more dim stars are visible. Your eyes have become accustomed to the dark, and you can see much better.

About how many stars do you see now? You may be

surprised to find out that a person with good eyesight can see only about two thousand stars even on the clearest night. You see far fewer than two thousand in the night sky of a brightly lit city.

But the hundreds of stars you can see even in a city are full of interest and fascination. Some of them appear to be blue or blue-white. Others may look red, yellow, or some other color. One star may be very close to another. Others are clustered in small groups.

Perhaps you are able to pick out a band of hazy light that stretches across the sky. The band of light is called the Milky Way. The Milky Way is made up of thousands and thousands of stars. But they are all so far away that your unaided eye sees them as only a patch of light.

You may be able to pick out a group of stars that seems to form a pattern. These patterns of stars are called *constellations*. You may see a few bright stars in the night sky that don't twinkle as the others do. These are probably not stars but planets such as Mars, Jupiter, Saturn, Mercury, and the brightest of all, Venus.

Imagine how you would have viewed the stars if you had lived hundreds of years ago. There were no electric lights, no radio or television, and few books. The nights were dark, lonely, and mysterious. At night the stars shone like points of fire in the dark dome of the sky. What could the stars be? Whatever they were, most people believed that they were the result of powers far beyond those of earth-bound humans.

Many legends and myths were made up about the stars. As they looked to the night sky, some people saw among the brighter stars figures of dragons and bears, hunters and kings, heroes and gods. They outlined these figures and gave them names. Naming the stars in the sky made them more familiar and less terrifying to the early star-watchers.

Centuries later, scientists still use many of these pictures in the night sky. We still use the stars as a calendar and as a direction finder. But now we know much more about the stars. We know that the stars are really giant balls of flaming gases much like our own sun but unimaginably farther away. We know that the planets circle around the sun in the same way our own planet earth does. We have visited the moon and sent space probes to nearby planets.

Yet we still marvel and wonder at the night sky. Here is how the English poet Byron felt when he saw the stars:

> *Who ever gazed upon them shining,*
> *And turned to earth without repining,*
> *Nor wished for wings to flee away,*
> *And mix with their eternal ray?*

Many poets and writers as well as scientists have

written of the stars. To understand the feeling they have for the stars, go out on a crisp, clear night and look to the sky.

This book will help you to pick out planets, stars, and constellations. It is not so much an astronomy book as an observing book. Whether you go outside to look at the stars for a few minutes or plan to spend many hours observing, use this book as your field guide to the night sky.

CHAPTER 1

WHEN
YOU GO OUT
TO OBSERVE

*N*o matter where you live—city, suburb, or out in the country—you can see some stars if the night is not too cloudy. But you'll see fewer stars when you observe near bright lights or in hazy or smoggy air.

All the conditions which interfere with your observing take place in the earth's atmosphere. If you were looking at the stars from a space ship or from our airless moon, you would have perfect observing conditions. The stars would be brilliant pinpoints of lights against a jet-black sky. They would shine steadily without twinkling.

But when you look at the sky from the street, a backyard, or a rooftop, you are viewing the stars through miles and miles of air. The air contains water droplets, dust particles, smoke, and other substances, which make

it difficult to see clearly and also cause the sky to glow
when they reflect streetlamps and other lights.

Winter nights are often clear and are excellent for observing. The air is usually dry, and strong winds keep
pollution from building up. Winter nights also begin
earlier in the evening, and often you can observe the stars
right after supper. Of course, winter nights may be very
cold, so you should bundle up.

Summer nights are warmer and more comfortable, and
when the weather is dry, the stars may be quite brilliant.
You'll have to wait until later at night to start observing, however. In some places, it doesn't get dark during
the early summer until well past 9:00 or 10:00 P.M.

A full moon will light up the sky and look very beautiful during any season. But the light of the moon will
also make it difficult to see any but the brightest stars.
Unless you want to observe the moon itself, it is best to
avoid observing on moonlit nights.

If you live in a city, you may have special problems
when you observe. Brightly lit downtown areas have so
much "sky glow" that only a few stars are visible. Auto
fumes, dust, smoke, and other pollutants may also build
up in a city and make observing difficult.

The amount of smog and air pollution in a city often
depends upon the weather. A good stiff wind or a heavy
rain can clear the air and make the next night good for
viewing. You just have to be prepared when a good view-

ing night comes along. Try to observe from a spot where nearby buildings screen off bright lights. You may see less of the sky, but the part that you see will show more stars.

If you live in the suburbs or out in the country, your observing problems are simpler. Just choose a clear, dry, moonless night. Observe from a backyard, school grounds, or open field. Find a place away from street lamps, or screen out the lights with trees or a building.

Wherever you observe, you'll see more stars if you adjust your eyes to the dark. Just close your eyes for several minutes, or keep from looking at a light until your eyes adapt. During the time you are adapting, the dark spot in the center of your eye (called the pupil) is enlarging to let in more light. Once you are dark-adapted, don't look directly at a flashlight, a street lamp, or any other bright light. If you do, you will lose your dark-adaptation quickly.

If you want to use a flashlight to find your way or to look at a star map, try this: Before you go out observing, wrap the head of a flashlight with several layers of red cellophane or some other transparent red material. Tape the red material in place so that it won't fall off easily. You can use the red light to look at things without losing your dark-adaptation.

When you are first learning to pick out the major constellations, it's not a bad idea to go out observing soon after sunset. Only the brighter stars and planets are visible in the early evening, and you won't be confused by many dimmer stars. Later in the evening, when the sky gets darker, you'll see the fainter stars and other faint sky objects.

If you are going to observe for a long period of time, try to make yourself comfortable. Standing upright and looking at stars high overhead is sure to give you a stiff neck. Lying on an old blanket or two spread on the ground, or on a reclining beach chair can be quite comfortable. Remember that it can get quite cold at night, so dress warmly. Bring along another blanket to cover yourself when you lie down.

The stars, constellations, planets, and other sky sights you see on any night depend upon the time of night and the month of the year. If you watch the night sky for a while, you'll see that the stars seem to move in the night sky. Some rise and some set as time goes on. Other stars seem to circle a star in the northern sky, called the North Star. The North Star appears not to move because it is almost directly above the earth's northern axis of rotation.

Stars seem to move during the night because of the earth's rotation, or turning on its axis. As the earth rotates, you and everybody else on our planet rotate with it. This makes it look to us as if the stars are moving. Of course, we are really the ones who are moving.

As the earth rotates, stars seem to rise in the east and set in the west. Later in the night you will see stars that are not visible during the earlier hours of the evening. The earth rotates once on its axis each day. Since a day is divided into twenty-four hours, the earth will rotate about one-third of a turn during an eight-hour night. This means that the stars will make about one-third of a complete circle during the night. The stars will make a greater fraction of a complete circle during a longer night.

As the earth rotates, it also revolves or travels around the sun. That trip takes one year to complete. During the earth's revolution around the sun, some stars will be hidden by the sun's bright light. We'll see those stars when the earth moves around to the other side of the sun, months later. That's why some stars and constellations are visible only during certain months of the year.

If all these nightly and monthly movements of the stars sound very confusing, don't be concerned. You can learn which stars are visible at any particular time of night in any particular month by using one of the star charts in this book. And there is no time, whether early or late in the evening, in summer, autumn, winter, or spring that some interesting sky sight is not there for you to view.

CHAPTER 2

MAPPING THE NIGHT SKY
THE POLE-CIRCLING CONSTELLATIONS

*O*NE star looks pretty much like any other star up in the night sky. Not only that, but a bright star that you see in one spot of the sky in the early evening is in a different spot a few hours later. How is it possible then to tell one star from another?

About the only way to identify a star is to look at it as part of a group of stars—a group that forms a picture or a pattern in the sky. People have been observing stars in this way for thousands of years. The groups or patterns of stars are called constellations. You'll be able to find a star by looking for it in or near a constellation.

You'll need a map to find a constellation in the same way you would need a map to find your way around an unfamiliar neighborhood. But once you've learned your way around a neighborhood you no longer need a map. And the same thing is true with the constellations.

When you use a city map, you start at a big street and find the smaller streets that branch off it. You don't pay attention to the cars and people that move around. In the night sky, you first find the bigger and easier constellations—then you look for the smaller ones nearby. You don't pay attention to the moon and the planets that change their position among the stars.

Some constellations are called by more than one name, and some drawings of constellations may connect the stars in different ways. But the stars are the same. In this book, we'll tell you all their names so that if you read about them in an astronomy book you'll know what constellations they are.

The first star to look for in the night sky is the North Star (*Polaris*). The North Star is nearly stationary in the sky. All of the other stars seem to circle around the North Star. The North Star is fairly bright but *not* the brightest star in the sky. It represents the end of the handle of a faint group of stars called the Little Dipper (*Ursa Minor*, or the Little Bear).

For thousands of years travelers have used the North Star to help guide them along their way. The North Star remains in the same position in the sky all night long,

THE
LITTLE DIPPER

North Star

while the other stars seem to circle around it. Just by relying on the North Star, early voyagers found their way across uncharted oceans and unexplored lands.

The best way to find the North Star is first to find the Big Dipper, a bright group of stars that looks just like a dipper. It is visible all night long from most places in the Northern Hemisphere. Draw an imaginary line between the two end stars in the bowl of the Big Dipper and continue the line until you come to the North Star.

THE BIG DIPPER

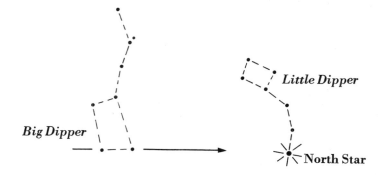

Big Dipper

Little Dipper

North Star

Astronomers say that the Big Dipper is not a constellation by itself. The Big Dipper is part of a constellation called the Big Bear (*Ursa Major*). To find the Big Bear, trace out the stars from the Big Dipper. The handle of the Dipper forms the upper head and neck of the Bear. The cup forms part of the Bear's back.

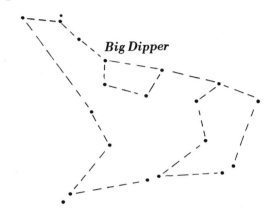

Big Dipper

THE BIG BEAR

As with most of the constellations, the Big Bear and the Little Bear were named after characters in Greek or Roman mythology. Here is the Roman myth that explains how the Bears came to be constellations:

Jupiter, the king of the gods, liked to flirt with beautiful women. Not only did he flirt with them, he often married them, despite the fact that he was married to Juno, the queen of the gods. Juno was unhappy at Jupiter's other marriages and often tried to harm his other wives.

One of Jupiter's wives, Callisto, bore him a son named Arcas. In anger, Juno punished Callisto by turning her into a bear and ordering her to roam the forests forever. Arcas grew up and became a hunter. One day while hunting in the forest, he tracked down a bear and was about to kill it. The bear was Callisto.

Jupiter, realizing what was happening, immediately turned Arcas into a small bear. Then Jupiter placed both bears in the night sky, where they roam close together to this day.

The Big Dipper is probably the easiest to spot and the most familiar of the constellations. Hundreds of years ago, the Arabs were supposed to have used it to test the eyesight of their scouts. See how you would do. Look at the next to the last star in the handle of the Dipper. Do you see one star or two? There are really two. The brighter one is named Mizar, and the fainter is named Alcor. In Arabic the names mean "the horse" and "the rider." If you can spot Alcor, you have good eyesight.

When you use the star maps in this book, remember that the constellations will be much, much larger when you see them in the night sky. Make sure you take your time when you look. If you can identify one or two constellations each evening when you observe, you are doing fine.

If you can't find the constellation you are looking for, remember that you can see every star in a constellation without turning your head. Just shift your eyes. Stick to the small part of the sky you are looking at until you find the group. If you become discouraged, stop and try again some other time.

The North Star is the axis or center point of a group of nearby constellations called the *pole-circling constellations* (or *circumpolar constellations*). The pole-circling constellations are visible, at least in part, at any hour of the night in any season to an observer in the United States or any country in the North Temperate Zone.

The stars in the Big Dipper are useful for finding some of the other pole-circling constellations. Draw an imaginary line from the handle star nearest the bowl of the Dipper to the North Star and an equal distance beyond. The line will reach a group of stars that look like an "M" or a "W." The W (*Cassiopeia*) is one of the many constellations that are named for people or animals in Greek myths. Think of the W stars as the points in a queen's crown.

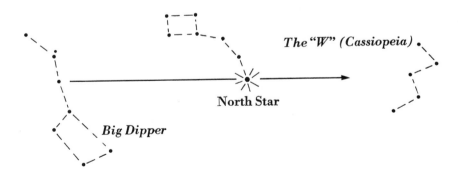

In between the Big and the Little Dippers are a few bright stars. These form the tail of a constellation called the Dragon (*Draco*). Follow the stars on around the bowl of the Little Dipper. A triangle of stars forms the head of the Dragon.

THE DRAGON

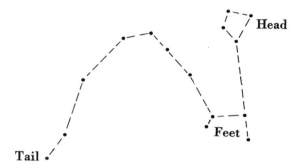

In between the Dragon and the W is the constellation called the King (*Cepheus*). The King's head is a rectangle, and he seems to be wearing a crown shaped like a dunce cap. This is not an easy constellation to find. In the autumn it is higher in the sky and easier to see.

THE KING

Cepheus (the King) and Cassiopeia (the W), along with two other constellations, Andromeda (the chained lady) and Perseus, are all part of the same Greek legend.

Cepheus and Cassiopeia were king and queen of Ethiopia, a country in Africa. Cassiopeia was so beautiful that all her subjects marveled at her. She boasted that she was even more beautiful than the sea nymphs.

Poseidon, the god of the sea, heard of Cassiopeia's boasting and was enraged. He sent a huge flood to cover the land, along with a giant sea monster that ravaged the countryside. To appease the god, Cepheus and Cassiopeia chained their only daughter, Andromeda, to a rock by the seashore.

Andromeda was rescued by Perseus, a Greek hero who had just cut off the head of the Medusa. The Medusa had snakes in place of hair, and anyone who looked at her would turn to stone. Perseus showed the head of the Medusa to the sea monster, which turned to stone. Naturally, Andromeda married Perseus as a reward. In the night sky, you can still see (if you have a good imagination) Perseus dangling the head of the dread Medusa.

Look also for some bright stars that are near the pole-circling constellations. Draw an imaginary line across the top of the Big Dipper and extend it until you reach a very bright star. Look at it for a while and you will notice that it appears yellow. This star is called *Capella*. It is the seventh brightest star in the sky. During the winter months, look for it directly over your head (at the zenith).

Big Dipper

Next draw a line from the bottom star in the bowl of the Big Dipper through the first star in the handle. You'll pass beyond the Dragon's head to a brilliant blue-white star called *Vega*. It is the fifth brightest star in the sky. On summer nights look for Vega directly overhead.

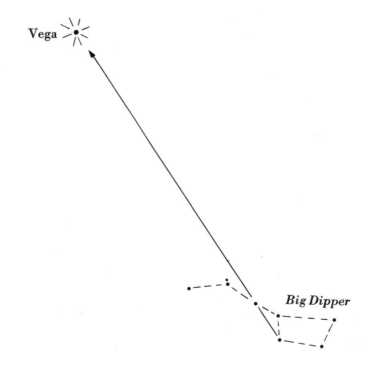

There is another pole-circling constellation called the Giraffe (*Camelopardalis*). But its stars are so dim that it is difficult to see even on clear nights. The handle of the Little Dipper points toward the Giraffe.

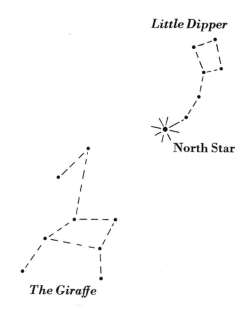

THE GIRAFFE

Little Dipper

North Star

The Giraffe

Here's a star map to help you to locate the pole-circling constellations. The more important and brighter stars are shown by this symbol ✳ . To use the chart, first face the North Star. Hold the chart in front of you so that the present month is on the top. That is how the constellations will look at 9:00 P.M. (10:00 P.M. daylight savings time). Turn the chart one month *clockwise* for every two hours before 9:00 P.M. Turn the chart one month *counterclockwise* for every two hours after 9:00 P.M.

THE POLE-CIRCLING
CONSTELLATIONS

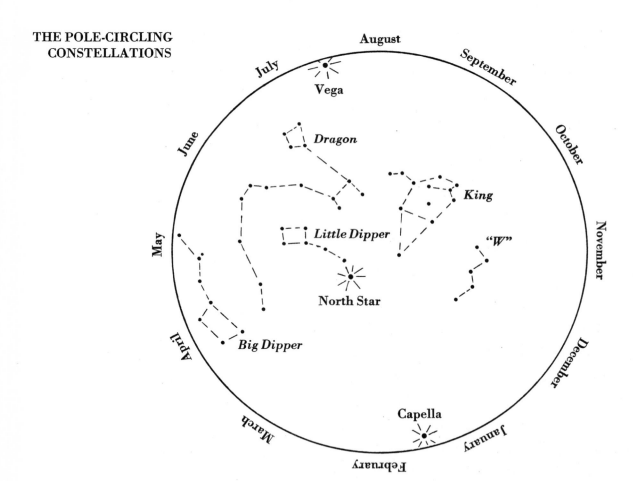

CHAPTER 3

AS
THE SEASONS
CHANGE

ALTHOUGH the stars of pole-circling constellations are always in view during the night, the other constellations are visible only at certain times. Some of the constellations are not too distant from the North Star and appear some time during the night most months of the year. Other constellations are farther from the North Star and are visible only during certain seasons.

The sun seems to follow the same path through the sky year after year. This pathway in the sky is called the *ecliptic*. Over the year, the path of the sun takes it through twelve constellations, called the *zodiac*. You can't see the constellation that the sun is in during the day because the bright light of the sun blots out all the stars. But you can see some of the zodiac constellations in the night sky. They rise and set during the night in the same way that the sun rises and sets in the day. At any one time you may be able to see four or five zodiac constellations in the night sky.

The twelve constellations were named long, long ago. They are the Bull (*Taurus*), the Twins (*Gemini*), the Crab (*Cancer*), the Lion (*Leo*), the Virgin (*Virgo*), the Scales (*Libra*), the Scorpion (*Scorpius*), the Archer (*Sagittarius*), the Goat (*Capricornus*), the Water Carrier (*Aquarius*), the Fishes (*Pisces*), and the Ram (*Aries*). At night, the moon and the planets travel through the zodiac constellations.

Some people think that the zodiac constellations and the planets which appear to move through them have an influence on human behavior. They try to predict what will happen on certain days and tell you how to behave on those days.

This kind of prediction is called *astrology*. Astrologers use the date and time of your birth and the position on that date of the stars, sun, moon, and planets to predict your character, your fate, and your future. The prediction is called your *horoscope*. Many newspapers carry a horoscope each day. If you want to find out about your horoscope turn to page 79.

Horoscopes are fun to do, but astrology does not meet the test of a true science. In order for a field of knowledge to be called a science it has to be able to tell *how* events are caused and to be able to repeat those events under the same conditions. Astrology uses observations but its predictions are not based on known facts. The science of the stars and planets is called *astronomy*. Don't confuse *astronomy* with *astrology*.

The constellations of the zodiac are nearer the horizon and to the south of the North Star. The other constellations mentioned below lie between the zodiac and the pole-circling constellations. Some of the constellations are filled with bright stars and are easy to spot. Others are more difficult to see. We'll tell you the best viewing month or season for each constellation.

Spring Constellations

The Lion (*Leo*) is a large zodiac constellation with two very bright stars, *Regulus* and *Denebola*. The best month for viewing it is April. Find Leo by drawing an imaginary line from the pointer stars in the Big Dipper and going the other way from the North Star. Draw another imaginary line from the other two stars in the bowl of the Dipper and they will point pretty close to Regulus.

Once you have located the Lion you can easily find a few other constellations that are visible most of the spring months. Look from the Lion back to the Big Dipper and then off to the east (your left as you look south). You'll see a constellation called the Herdsman

THE LION

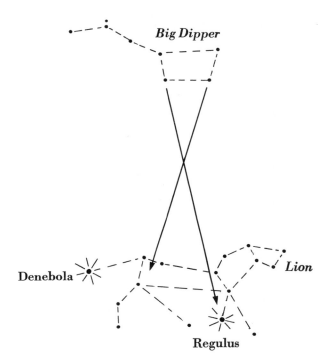

(*Boötes*). Use your imagination to see the Herdsman smoking a pipe. The fourth brightest star in the sky, called *Arcturus,* is in the Herdsman.

Travel back from the Herdsman through the Big Dipper to find a constellation called the Twins (*Gemini*). The Twins is a zodiac constellation that is best seen in

February and early spring. The Twins are so named because of the bright stars in each of their heads. The stars are named *Pollux* and *Castor*.

On the opposite side of the Lion from the Twins is the zodiac constellation called the Virgin (*Virgo*). May is the best month to see the Virgin. *Spica* is a bright star in the Virgin. Find Spica by drawing an imaginary arc through the handle of the Big Dipper through Arcturus and then to Spica. Spica is the only bright star in that part of the sky. The rest of the constellation is made up of faint stars difficult to see.

In early times, it was often the custom to plant crops or to harvest them according to the appearance of certain stars in the sky. Most often, the best time was judged to be when a particular star appeared on the eastern horizon just before sunrise. The first rising of Spica or the whole constellation of the Virgin was a signal that the planting of wheat should begin.

On the next page is a map of the main springtime constellations. Look to the south to see them (to the opposite horizon from the North Star).

Summer Constellations

Summer is a pleasant season for star observing. The weather is warmer, and you may be enjoying a vacation and have time on your hands. Though the summer sky

SPRINGTIME CONSTELLATIONS

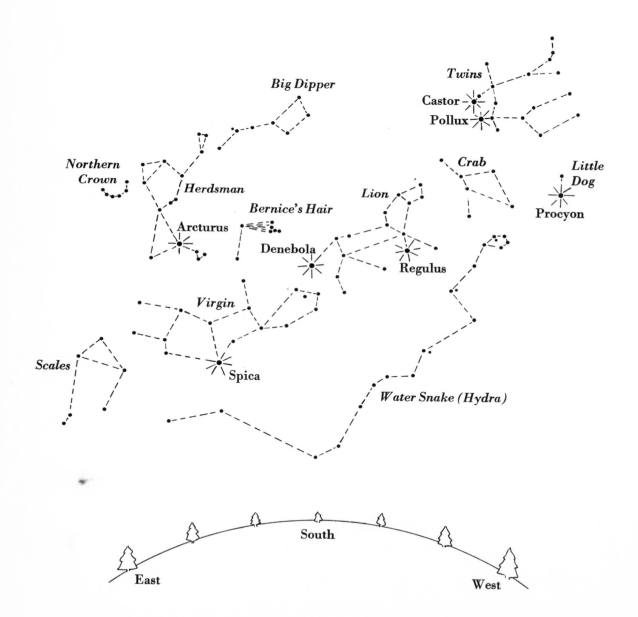

does not contain as many bright stars or easy-to-spot constellations as the spring sky, the Milky Way is very impressive during the summer.

The Milky Way is a huge mass of millions and millions of stars. The stars are so far away that we can't see them as individual points of light without a telescope. Instead, they blend together in a band of hazy light that stretches across the night sky from the southeast to the northeast. You can see the Milky Way on any clear, moonless night of the year. But the Milky Way is brightest during late summer.

To see the Milky Way best, you have to observe it from a place far from street lights or city sky glow. Dark-adapt your eyes (see page 7) to see it even more clearly. What you are really looking at is a sort of edge view of an enormous group of stars called a *galaxy*. Our sun is part of the Milky Way galaxy, out toward one edge. When we look at the Milky Way in the night sky, we are looking toward the many stars in the center of the galaxy.

The Milky Way is not the only galaxy in the universe. There are millions of others, each containing billions of stars. Most of them are too faint to be seen without a telescope. But you can see others with your unaided eye or with a pair of low-power binoculars.

Start to locate the summer constellations by spotting a late springtime constellation, the Herdsman. As you look to the south at an early hour on a summer evening, the Herdsman is midway between the horizon and the zenith to your right (west). A little to the left of the Herdsman is a bright semicircle of seven stars that form a sort of crown. This is called the Northern Crown (*Corona Borealis*). The crown is supposed to be the gift the god Bacchus gave to Ariadne when he married her. Use the handle of the Big Dipper to point your way to the Crown.

Continuing left (east) you may see a large square made up of four rather dim stars. This is the square of the constellation Hercules—notice the large club he's carrying. It was used by Hercules to kill a large man-eating lion. Still farther left (east) is a large triangle made up of three very bright stars. Each one is part of a different constellation.

Closest to Hercules is the fifth brightest star in the sky, *Vega*. Vega is in the constellation called the Lyre (*Lyra*). A lyre is an ancient stringed musical instrument. The lyre in the sky belonged to Orpheus, the most marvelous musician who ever lived. A little higher in the sky and farther to the left of Vega is the bright star *Deneb*. Deneb is in the constellation called the Swan (*Cygnus*), sometimes called the Northern Cross. If you can imagine water pouring out of the cup of the Big Dipper, it would splash on the Swan just past the Little Dipper.

Down toward the southern horizon from Deneb is the bright star called *Altair*. It is part of the constellation

SUMMERTIME CONSTELLATIONS

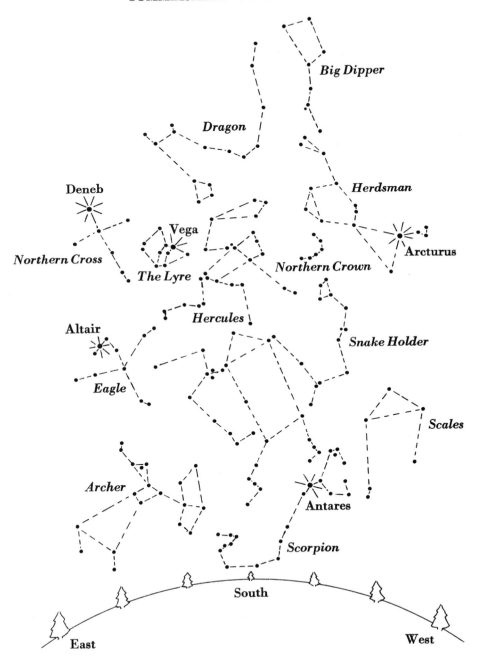

called the Eagle (*Aquila*). Down toward the horizon from the swan and a bit to the right (west) is another bright star called *Antares*. If you look at Antares closely you will see that it is definitely reddish in color. Antares is part of the zodiac constellation called the Scorpion (*Scorpius*). It is best seen during the month of July.

The Scorpion is always rising while the constellation of the Hunter, *Orion*, is always setting. This is only reasonable. The Scorpion stung and killed the Hunter in the legend. You wouldn't expect Jupiter to place them next to each other in the sky.

Autumn Constellations

As autumn begins, the springtime constellations have disappeared from the night sky. The pole-circling constellations have made a half turn around the North Star. The Big Dipper is low on the northern horizon, while the W is well up in the northern sky. The constellations of early autumn have few bright stars and are difficult to identify. But autumn nights are often crisp and clear and the observing is good.

Begin to identify the new constellations by locating the North Star, the W, and the King. Now draw an imaginary line southward from the North Star. Continue the line between the W and the King until you reach a large square made up of four bright stars. This is the Great

AUTUMN CONSTELLATIONS

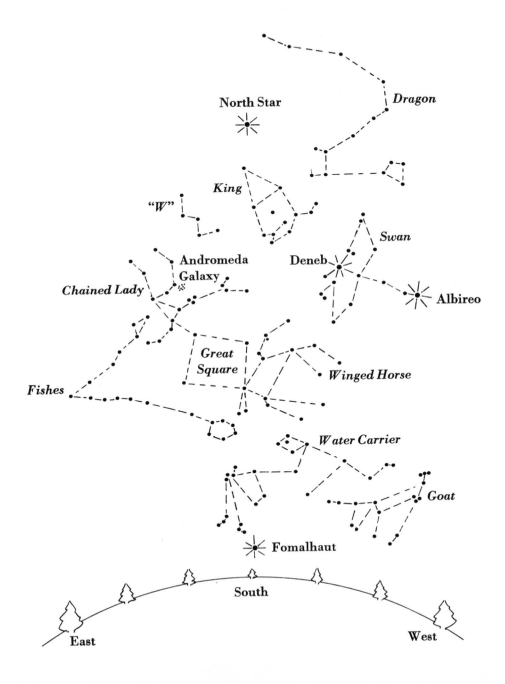

North Star

Dragon

King

"W"

Swan

Deneb

Andromeda
Galaxy

Albireo

Chained Lady

*Great
Square*

Winged Horse

Fishes

Water Carrier

Goat

Fomalhaut

South

East

West

Square of the Winged Horse (*Pegasus*). The square makes up the wing of the Horse.

Between the Great Square and the W is the constellation called the Chained Lady (*Andromeda*). For the story of the Chained Lady see page 17. This looks like two long lines of stars. Just to the side of these lines is a faint spot of light. This spot is a distant galaxy similar to the Milky Way galaxy. (See page 71 on how to observe this galaxy.) When you see this light you are looking across two-million light-years of space. (One light-year is the distance light travels in one year—5.8 trillion miles.) It is the most distant object you can see in the sky without using binoculars or a telescope.

Below the Chained Lady and left (east) of the Great Square is the zodiac constellation called the Fishes (*Pisces*). Below the Fishes and a bit right (west) is the zodiac constellation called the Water Carrier (*Aquarius*). To the right of the Water Carrier is the zodiac constellation called the Goat (*Capricornus*). All of these are faint constellations that are difficult to make out. But you may see a bright star just south of the Water Carrier. It is *Fomalhaut,* a star in the constellation called the Southern Fish (*Piscis Austrinus*).

Winter Constellations

After the dim and difficult-to-spot constellations of the autumn sky, the winter sky is a treat. It contains some of the brightest stars in the night sky and the most beautiful constellation of all, the Hunter (Orion).

Look to the southern horizon during December for three bright stars, close together and in a row. These form the Hunter's belt. The left shoulder and the right leg of the Hunter are marked by two very bright stars, *Betelgeuse* (pronounced "beetle juice" by most amateur astronomers) and *Rigel*. Betelgeuse is a red star and Rigel is a brilliant blue-white star.

These two are by no means the only bright stars in the winter sky. Naturally, all good hunters must have a dog to help them, and Orion is no exception. Draw a line to the left (southeast) through the stars in the Hunter's belt. You will come to the brightest star in the sky, *Sirius*, the Dog Star. It is in the constellation of the Big Dog (*Canis Major*).

Now draw a line back from Sirius through the belt of the Hunter and an equal distance on the other side. You'll reach a very bright red star called *Aldebaran*. It will be in a V-shaped group of stars in the zodiac constellation called the Bull (*Taurus*). There is a beautiful little group of stars in the Bull called the *Pleiades*. (More about them on page 71.)

Now go back to the Hunter and go straight left (east) from Betelgeuse. You'll reach another very bright star called *Procyon*. It is part of a small constellation called the Little Dog (*Canis Minor*). Sirius, Betelgeuse, and

WINTER CONSTELLATIONS

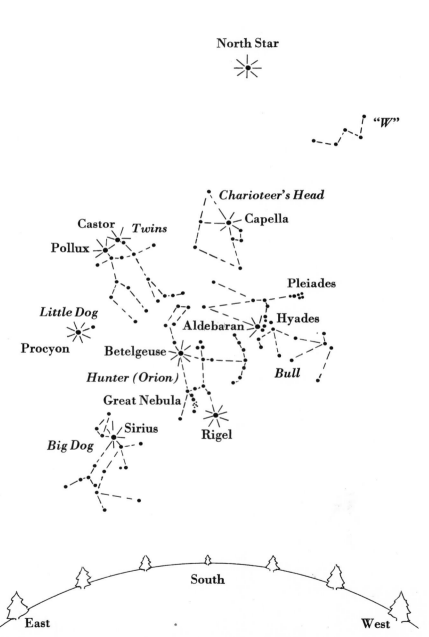

North Star

"W"

Charioteer's Head

Capella

Castor

Twins

Pollux

Pleiades

Little Dog

Aldebaran

Hyades

Procyon

Betelgeuse

Hunter (Orion)

Bull

Great Nebula

Sirius

Rigel

Big Dog

South

East

West

Procyon form a brilliant triangle of stars in the winter sky.

Also visible in the late winter sky are the bright stars of the Twins, Castor and Pollux. Still another bright star visible in the winter is Capella in the constellation called the Charioteer's Head (*Auriga*). Find Capella between the W and the Twins.

The constellations we have shown and described are by no means the only constellations visible in the Northern Hemisphere. But they are the easiest to spot and will give you a start in finding your way among the stars.

CHAPTER 4

HOW
TO FIND
THE PLANETS

THE chances are that you have seen one of the planets in the night sky many times. *Venus* is far brighter than the brightest star. *Mars, Jupiter,* and *Saturn* are also very bright at times during the year.

Mercury can also be bright. But it is so close to the sun it is only visible close to the horizon just before the sun rises or just after the sun sets. The outer three planets, *Uranus, Neptune,* and *Pluto,* are too faint to see without a telescope.

You may have seen a planet, but how can you tell a planet from a star? For one thing, the stars remain in the same positions each year. (Actually, even the stars move about. But because the stars are so much more distant than the planets, it would take many thousands of years to notice their movements.) The planets seem to change their positions among the stars as the nights go by. The word "planet" comes from a Greek word which means "a wanderer."

So if you see a bright star that does not appear on a constellation chart, you may be looking at a planet. Here are some other ways to tell a planet. The planets, the sun, and the moon all move in the same general path across the sky called the *ecliptic*. So you can find the planets if you look at the night sky along the same path that the moon travels. The planets will always be in or near a zodiac constellation.

That means that if a bright star is near the North Star, it cannot be a planet. Planets never come even close to the North Star. If you are observing during the summer from the northern half of the United States or Europe, or any place in Canada, any visible planet will be low in the southern sky. In the winter, the planets may be seen much higher in the sky.

Except when they are high overhead, stars twinkle when you stare at them. The planets you can see shine so brightly that they usually do not twinkle. Venus is some-times so bright that it will cast your shadow behind you on a dark, moonless night.

The planets have different colors when you look at them, particularly if you use a small telescope or a pair of binoculars. Venus looks silvery, Mars looks reddish,

Jupiter looks white, and Saturn looks yellowish. When two planets are close together in the night sky, you can often tell them apart by their color. Jupiter and Mars appear to be about the same brightness, while Saturn is a bit less bright. Venus is much brighter than any of them.

To find out exactly where to look at any particular time you need an almanac for the year. Some daily newspapers will also list the positions of the planets. Just as an example, the almanac for October 1980 will list Venus as being in the constellation of the Lion, Jupiter and Saturn in the constellation of the Virgin, and Mars in the constellation of the Scorpion. Usually you can get more detailed observing information from a local astronomy club or a nearby planetarium or natural history museum.

You can observe the movements among the stars of the four brightest planets with your unaided eyes. But to look at them in any detail, a small telescope or a pair of binoculars will be very helpful. When you use a telescope or binoculars, it's a good idea to support them on a steady mount. If you do not have a tripod, use the back of a chair or a wooden box. Hand-held binoculars or a telescope will make the planets appear to jiggle as you look at them.

You may be surprised when you look at Venus. It shows changes in its shape, called *phases*, just as the moon does. When Venus is at its brightest, it will be in its first or last quarter phase. As it becomes less bright, it will become smaller but more nearly full. The brightness changes because Venus is closer to earth at some times and farther away at others. The phases occur for similar reasons to those of the moon. But no matter when you see Venus, it will show a disc, not just a spot of light, when viewed through a telescope.

Venus is seen near the horizon in the early evening or in the early morning. At these times it is sometimes called "the morning star" or "the evening star." Venus is named for the goddess of beauty. It is the brightest object in the sky except for the sun and the moon.

Mars will appear in the night sky at times very different from Venus. At certain times, Mars will rise at sunset and be visible all night long. At other times, it rises at midnight and can be seen only for several hours. Mars was named for the god of war.

If you observe Mars every night for a week or two, you will be able to see it change position against the background of stars. Most of the year, Mars moves rapidly eastward among the stars. But when it reaches a certain position, Mars begins to move backwards (west) for a few months. The changes in the motion of Mars are caused by the movement of the earth as well as that of Mars.

Mars looks orange-red through binoculars or a small telescope. You will be able to see a small disc, but don't bother looking for details on the surface of Mars. For one thing, the disc is too small. For another, the so-called

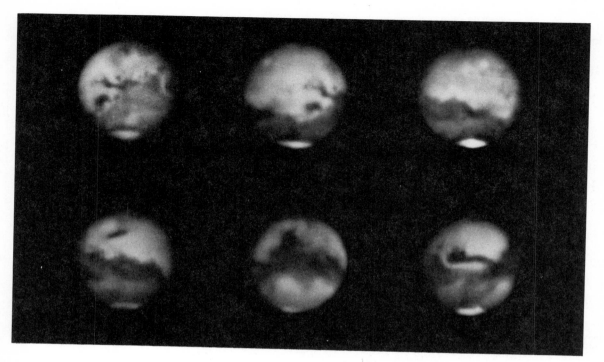

These photos of Mars were taken at different times of the Martian year. They clearly show seasonal changes in the polar cap and in the dark and light areas on the surface of the planet.

canals of Mars are really craters and other features much like those of our moon.

Jupiter is second only to Venus in brightness. You can see Jupiter in the morning sky about five months of each year and in the evening sky five months. The other two months, Jupiter is hidden by the sun's glare. Jupiter will always show a small disc through binoculars or a telescope. At times, you may even be able to see the four faint points of light that are the largest of Jupiter's moons. The moons are named after Jupiter's wives. The moons were

first seen by the great scientist Galileo with a small telescope over 350 years ago.

Saturn is the most distant of the planets known to the
early star-watchers. You would need binoculars or a telescope to see the last three planets in the solar system,
Uranus, Neptune, and Pluto.

Saturn takes many years to circle the sun, so it appears
to move very slowly among the stars. You can see it in the
same constellation for a year or longer. For example,
Saturn is in the constellation of the Lion all of 1978 and
most of 1979. The last three months of 1979 and all of

Even with a small telescope you can see some of the dark and light bands
that cross the face of Jupiter. The light-colored oval just below the
equator is called the "Great Red Spot." Scientists are still not sure of its
exact nature.

Saturn has a magnificent system of rings circling its banded surface. First observed by Galileo in 1610, the solid-looking rings are now believed to be made up of swarms of tiny particles, ranging in size from fine dust to coarse gravel.

1980, you can see Saturn in the constellation of the Virgin.

Through binoculars or a small telescope, Saturn doesn't have much of a disc and is not very interesting. Through a somewhat more powerful telescope you can see a disc and what look like bumps. Through a large telescope, you can see that the bumps are really rings that encircle the planet. And if you ever have a chance to look through a really large astronomical telescope, you will see that Saturn's rings are one of the most spectacular of all sights in the night sky.

CHAPTER 5

OBSERVING THE MOON

No need to tell you how to spot the moon. You've seen it late at night, early in the evening, and even during daylight hours. You've seen the moon as a full, round circle of light, bright enough to cast shadows of trees, buildings, and people. You've seen the moon as a thin, silvery crescent surrounded by stars. You've seen the moon many times. But have you ever really *observed* the moon carefully? Have you ever wondered why the moon changes its shape each month?

Because of the earth's rotation on its axis, the moon, like the sun and the stars, appears to rise in the east and set in the west. But the moon also revolves around the earth from west to east about once a month (or *moonth*). The result of these two movements is that the moon rises and sets anytime from thirty to seventy-five minutes later each day. The exact times for each moonrise and moonset are given by most daily newspapers.

The newspapers also will tell you what shape the moon is in, its *phase*. It takes just a little more than twenty-nine and one-half days for the moon to go through its phases. Here's why the moon has phases:

The moon doesn't shine by its own light as the sun and the stars do. The moon shines because it reflects the light of the sun. We can only see the part that is lighted by the sun. The rest looks dark.

When the moon is between the earth and the sun, the sunlight falls on the side of the moon facing away from us. The side facing the earth is dark, and we can't see it. This phase is called the new moon.

Each day the moon moves farther in its orbit around the earth. The side facing the earth begins to be lighted up. You can see a curved sliver called the crescent moon. We say that the moon is "waxing" (growing larger) because it is showing more and more of its face. A waxing crescent moon sets a few hours after the sun.

Each night the lighted part of the moon grows in size. Seven or eight days after the new moon, the moon looks like a half-circle. It is called the first-quarter moon because it is one quarter of the way around its orbit. You can see a first-quarter moon high in the sky during the afternoon. It shines the first part of the evening, setting in the middle of the night.

As the moon continues to wax it is called a gibbous moon. Finally the moon grows into a whole circle. When you see the whole face of the moon, it is a full moon. The full moon rises about sunset and sets about sunrise. It is very bright, blotting out all but the brightest stars.

As the moon moves on in its orbit around the earth, it begins to show less and less of its face. We say that the moon is "waning," or growing smaller. It passes through the gibbous phase again.

A bit more than three weeks after the new moon, the moon looks like a half-circle again. This is called the third- or last-quarter moon. A last-quarter moon rises in the middle of the night and sets around noontime. From last quarter, the moon wanes back to crescent and then to new moon.

You can see some of the moon's surface features, such as the dark and light areas, with your unaided eyes. But a pair of binoculars or a small telescope will show you much, much more. In fact, a pair of binoculars will show you so much detail on the moon that you may become confused at all you see.

The first thing to remember is that you will always be looking at the same side of the moon. The first time that anyone on the earth saw the other side of the moon was when pictures were taken from an unmanned space probe. Since then, of course, manned space ships have circled the moon, and human eyes have looked at the other side.

But because you see only one side of the moon, once you identify a feature on the moon's surface, you'll find it in the same place every time you look. Surprisingly, the full moon is not the best time to observe most of the moon's features. At full moon, the surface of the moon is brightly lit but appears flat and without shadows.

The best time to observe the moon is at one of the quarters. The sunlight is now striking the moon's surface at an angle, so each surface bump and hollow stands out clearly. The best place to look is where daylight and darkness meet on the moon's surface. Astronomers call this the *terminator* line.

At the terminator line, mountains, craters, plains, and valleys stand out sharply. As you observe the moon, you suddenly realize that you are really looking at another world in space. It is the only world close enough to study in detail even with low-power binoculars.

Try to look at the moon each clear night as it goes through its phases. Watch the terminator line creep across the surface of the moon, lighting up new mountain ranges and vast craters. Use the map of the moon on page 49 to help you identify what you see. Before long you'll be able to see much more than "the man in the moon."

Surface Features on the Moon

Remember that many features of the moon were named by early astronomers who thought the moon to be much like the earth. What they called oceans or seas or lakes we now know to be nothing of the sort. The moon is a dead world, without air or water or life. Despite what we know, we still use the old names for many places on the moon.

Seas (or *maria,* which is Latin for seas) are large, dark plains that cover much of the moon's surface. The seas form what looks like a person's face when you look at the moon without binoculars. Some of the seas are hundreds of miles across. They are flat and have few craters on their surfaces. Similar areas on the moon are sometimes named oceans or lagoons.

Craters are sprinkled over the moon's surface by the thousands (you'll see even more when you look with a larger telescope). Some places have many craters; other places not so many. The largest of the craters is over 100 miles in diameter. The smallest are just a few inches across and can only be seen by space probes. Astronomers think that most of the craters were caused by the impact of meteorites, chunks of rock and iron in space (see chapter six).

Some of the largest craters, such as *Copernicus* and *Tycho,* have mountain peaks in their center. The peaks may rise thousands of feet from the crater floor. Other large craters, such as *Plato,* are filled with a smooth dark material like that of the moon's seas.

Mountains and Mountain Ranges on the moon often

See how many features on the surface of the moon you can pick out, using the map on the facing page. South appears at the top.

surround the seas or plains. Some are very high. They are as tall as the highest mountain ranges on the earth.

Rays are bright lines or streaks radiating outward from some of the larger craters. The rays are more easily seen during full moon than at other phases. Some of the rays coming out of the crater Tycho are over one thousand miles long. In fact, the ray system of Tycho makes the full moon look something like a peeled orange.

Rays probably form when a meteorite hits the moon's surface and makes a crater. In the great explosion, masses of moon rock are flung out. These crash to the ground and

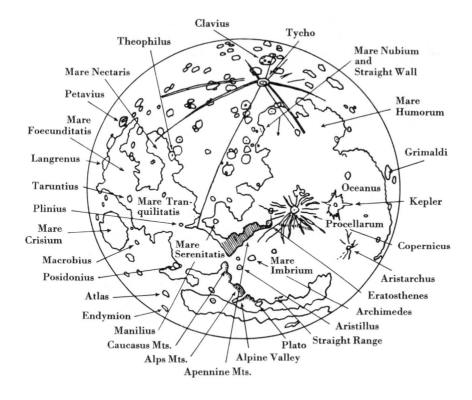

Clavius · Tycho · Theophilus · Mare Nubium and Straight Wall · Mare Nectaris · Mare Humorum · Petavius · Mare Foecunditatis · Grimaldi · Langrenus · Oceanus · Kepler · Taruntius · Mare Tranquilitatis · Plinius · Procellarum · Mare Crisium · Copernicus · Mare Serenitatis · Macrobius · Mare Imbrium · Aristarchus · Posidonius · Eratosthenes · Atlas · Archimedes · Endymion · Aristillus · Manilius · Straight Range · Caucasus Mts. · Plato · Alps Mts. · Alpine Valley · Apennine Mts.

form smaller craters around the main crater. At the same time, large amounts of fine dust stream out from the impact point, forming long splashes or rays.

Other features of the moon's surface include valleys, ringed plains, rills or clefts, and domes. Ringed plains are circular craters with high mountains all around them. At full moon, some of the ringed plains such as Copernicus and Tycho look much brighter than at other times. Rills are long, narrow valleys. Many rills are separate; others are parts of groups.

CHAPTER 6

COMETS
AND
METEORS

"EARTH to Pass Through Comet's Tail" read the newspaper headlines many years ago. Some people became very frightened at what might happen. They even thought that the world was coming to an end.

On May 19, 1910, the earth passed directly into the tail of Halley's comet. What happened? Nothing. Here's why: The tail of a comet is made up of wispy gases. The gases are so thin that a comet's tail a million miles long could be compressed into a suitcase. One astronomer joked that the tail of Halley's comet was just a big bag of airy nothing.

Comets, like planets, revolve around the sun. But the orbits of comets are long ovals, something like the shape of an egg. At one end of its path, a comet may pass very near the sun. At the other end it may be very far away, at the limits of the solar system.

Far out in its orbit, a comet is nothing more than a small collection of stone and metal chips, ice, dust, and gases, about one or two miles across. In the distant reaches of space, a comet is dark, solid, and frozen. A comet is sometimes described as a kind of large, dirty snowball.

But as a comet moves in its orbit closer to the sun, its material begins to melt and turn into gas. The gases expand and begin to glow in the light of the sun. A head of glowing gases like a halo forms around the frozen core.

As the comet comes still closer to the sun, the ball of glowing gases becomes very large. It may measure hundreds of thousands, even one million miles across. The gases that make up the head of a comet are so thin and light that the sun's rays and particles push them away from the head. That's how a comet's tail forms. The tail always points away from the sun. When a comet approaches the sun, its tail streams behind or to one side. But when a comet moves away from the sun, the tail goes first.

The orbits of comets are of different sizes. Some comets take a few years to make their journeys around the sun. Some take tens or hundreds of years. Others take thousands of years and may never return again.

Each year, perhaps ten comets return to the neighborhood of the sun. You would need a telescope to see most of them. Only rarely is a comet big and bright enough to be seen without a telescope. Perhaps the most famous of these large comets is Halley's. (Edmund Halley was the first astronomer to explain the way in which comets move.) Halley's comet orbits the sun in about seventy-five or seventy-six years. It was last seen in 1910. At this moment it is making its return trip to the sun. We should be able to see it in 1985 or 1986.

If you can use a small telescope and want to see a comet, you need first to find its exact location when it is visible. Magazines such as *Sky and Telescope* or yearly guides such as *The Observer's Handbook* will supply the information you need. Most comets will appear as little more than a tiny spot or patch of light.

A few new comets are discovered every year. They may be newly formed comets or just comets that no one ever noticed before. Nobody knows for sure.

Even familiar comets change and do not last forever. One bright comet came back and developed two tails rather than a single tail. Another broke up as it was being observed. On each trip around the sun a comet loses some of its gas and other material. Nothing is left except the rock and dust particles. The particles go on orbiting the sun. Sometimes the earth passes through a swarm of these particles. They enter our atmosphere and we are treated to a meteor shower.

HALLEY'S COMET IN 1910

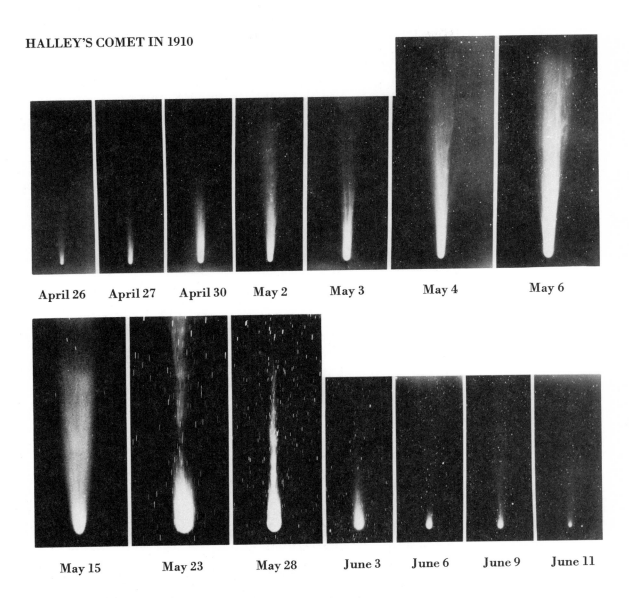

April 26   April 27   April 30   May 2   May 3   May 4   May 6

May 15   May 23   May 28   June 3   June 6   June 9   June 11

These views of Halley's comet clearly show how a comet increases in
size as it approaches the sun.

Meteors

If you look at the night sky, you are far more likely to see a meteor than a comet. A meteor looks like a sudden streak of light that flashes across the sky. Some people call it a "shooting star." Of course a meteor is not a star, nor does it shoot anything.

Meteors are usually tiny bits of rock or dust particles. Most are no larger than the nail on your little finger. These pieces are moving with great speed. When they enter the earth's atmosphere the pieces become red hot and begin to glow. We see them only for the few seconds that they are glowing.

Try this: Rub your hands together slowly a few times. Now rub your hands together as quickly as you can. You can feel your hands becoming much hotter at the greater speed.

Out in space there is no atmosphere for the tiny particles to rub against. But they begin to rub against molecules of air when they come near the earth. Meteors move very, very fast. They travel at speeds faster than that of a bullet shot from a gun. You can see why they get so hot when they rub against air molecules.

On any night of the year, some meteors can be seen. Away from the sky glow of city lights, and with clear sky conditions, you can see an average of seven meteors per hour. A full moon, bright lights, or a hazy sky will reduce the number you see. You can see more meteors in the early morning hours than in the evening.

At certain times during the year you can see many more meteors per hour. These so-called meteor showers happen when the earth passes through the remains of a comet.

Some meteor showers take place each year at about the same date. Each shower seems to come from the direction of a particular constellation. Therefore the meteor shower is named for the constellation.

For example, on the night of August 12 each year, a meteor shower looks as if it is coming from the direction of the constellation Perseus. It is called the *Perseid* shower. It goes on all night. You may be able to see as many as fifty meteors per hour.

Here are the approximate dates of some of the larger yearly meteor showers. You may not be able to see all of them each year. If it is daylight in your area when the earth passes through the meteor swarm, then you won't be able to see them at all.

Shower	*Approximate Date*		*Rate per hour*	
Quadrantids	January	3	40	(These rates include the
Lyrids	April	22	15	seven meteors per hour you
Perseids	August	12	50	can see on any night)
Orionids	October	21	25	
Taurids	November	4	15	
Leonids	November	16	15	
Geminids	December	13	50	

Most meteors burn up fifty or sixty miles above the earth's surface. A great many enter the atmosphere day and night. Some scientists say the number is close to 100 million every day. From time to time, a much larger meteor arrives. It makes a flash of light brighter than the stars and planets. We call it a *fireball*. It may even look like a round, glowing ball with a tail.

If the meteor is even larger, it may not burn up in the earth's atmosphere. It makes a brilliant streak in the sky and then falls to the earth's surface. A meteor that reaches the earth's surface is called a *meteorite*.

Most meteorites are tiny bits or chunks of rock. Some are larger, perhaps as big as your hand. Very rarely a meteorite may be larger than a person. You can see these very large meteorites in some museums and planetariums.

When a really huge meteorite strikes the earth, it hits like a bomb and leaves an enormous crater. Thousands of years ago such a meteorite fell in Arizona. The crater that it left is large enough to bury a small town.

CHAPTER 7

BUYING
AND USING
A TELESCOPE

SOONER or later you may decide that you want to buy a telescope to help you to observe the stars and the planets. Here's some information about how much they cost and to help you decide what kind to get.

A reasonably good, small astronomical telescope will cost from about fifty or sixty dollars on upward to several hundreds of dollars. Even the lower price range will buy you a telescope, plus a tripod for mounting it, that will let you observe many, many sky sights invisible to your unaided eye.

There are two different kinds of telescopes that are usually used in astronomy. Each gathers light from the stars or planets in a different way.

Refractors are telescopes that gather light by means of a lens at the front end of a tube. The lens is made of carefully ground and polished glass. Light rays that pass through the lens are bent in such a way that they come together at the other end of the tube. *Reflectors* gather light by means of a curved mirror at the bottom of a tube. The light is reflected back to a smaller mirror and then to a side opening.

Both kinds of telescopes direct the light rays into a small lens through which you look, called an *eyepiece*. The eyepiece spreads the light and makes the image appear bigger. The image appears upside down in both kinds of telescopes. In astronomy an upside-down image doesn't make any difference. You can study the moon or a planet just as well one way as the other. Turning the image right side up would mean using another lens, thus increasing the expense.

Each kind of telescope has certain advantages and disadvantages for amateur astronomers. Refractors are closed at both ends and are easier to keep clean than reflectors. Also, it is usually lightweight, portable, and easier to set up than a comparably priced reflector. A reasonably well-cared-for refractor can last for a lifetime.

A more modern (and much more expensive) telescope is a combination of a lens and mirrors. It is called a *catadioptric* telescope. These feature sealed tubes, superb seeing, and small size for easy carrying and setting up. Their only disadvantage is their high price. The least expensive catadioptric telescope costs over 500 dollars.

Many high schools and colleges own catadioptric telescopes. They are such a joy to use that it would be worth your while to find out if your local school has one or could afford to purchase one. They will reward viewers many times over their initial cost. Page 82 has a list of sources for catadioptrics, refractors, and reflectors.

While small-lens refractors are not too expensive, refractors with a lens 75 millimeters (about three inches) or larger are quite costly. It is very expensive to make a big, good lens. One problem is that the image seems to be surrounded by different colors. Another problem is that the image at the edges often is slightly distorted or bent.

Making a lens that deals with these problems increases the cost greatly. That's why you can buy the same size refractors for widely different prices. The more expensive refractors usually use better lenses in their construction.

Reflectors are much less expensive than the same size refractors. You can buy a 75- or 100-millimeter (three or four inches) reflector for about the same price as a refractor that is only half the diameter. The larger the telescope, the greater the price difference between reflectors and refractors.

But most reflectors have some disadvantages. Reflectors usually are open-ended. Dust and moisture can easily get

in and reach the mirror. The mirrors get out of adjustment more easily than lenses and need to be aligned
properly. From time to time (though rarely more often
than every few years) the mirrors may have to be re-
silvered or realuminized. But with some care you can
easily overcome these difficulties and learn to use a small
reflector.

A larger lens or mirror gathers more light than a
smaller one. It forms a brighter image. The eyepiece is
the lens that enlarges the image. But very high power
(called *magnification*) is exactly what you don't want as a
beginner in astronomy. The higher the power, the smaller
the area that you see in the scope. The smaller the area,
the more difficult it is to find an object in the sky. Most
of the time you will be using the lowest available power
in your scope, no more than 15x or 25x magnification.
That is, you would see the object fifteen to twenty-five
times larger in the telescope than you would with your
eyes alone.

Most telescopes come with different eyepieces so that
you can change the magnification you are using. As a
practical limit you would not use more than 50x magnification for each 25 millimeters of lens or mirror in your
scope. For example, a 50-millimeter scope could use up to
100x magnification, while a 100-millimeter scope could
use up to 200x. You would not gain any more detail by
using a higher power.

Which kind of telescope is best for you? For a young beginner, a small refractor that comes with a tripod is probably best. It is easy to use and to set up. It requires very little care to keep it in good working condition. Use it with magnification of 15x or 20x and you will have little difficulty in spotting the objects you are looking for.

If you are going to have an adult help you, then a small reflector telescope may be the best bet. For the same price as a small refractor you can get a much larger reflector. But either kind will give you many hours of enjoyable viewing.

It is very important to use a firm and steady mount when you use your scope. Most small astronomical scopes are sold complete with a wooden tripod. This should be set up so that you can move the telescope to follow the object that you are observing. The more expensive the telescope, usually the better the tripod that is supplied.

The kind of tripod that allows you to move the scope in all directions is called an *altazimuth mount*. It is the kind that comes with almost all less expensive scopes. It has one disadvantage. In order to follow a star for any length of time longer than a minute or two, you must make both vertical (up and down) and horizontal (side to side) adjustments by hand. The better (and more expensive) kinds of altazimuth mounts have fine-adjustment knobs that allow you to move the scope just by turning them.

The most expensive scopes may come equipped with a more complicated mounting called an *equatorial mount.* After you set up an equatorial mount properly, you need make only one adjustment to keep the object in view. This kind of mount is only for advanced amateur astronomers.

You can usually buy some extra accessories for your telescope if you decide you need them. A *Barlow lens* can be attached ahead of your eyepiece in the scope. It can double or triple the power of the eyepiece in use. Another kind of lens usually called an *image erector* will turn the upside-down image in your scope right side up. This will make your scope useful for observing objects around you on the earth but will be of no help in astronomy observing.

Before you buy a telescope you may be interested in finding out if there are any astronomy clubs nearby. Check your local schools or library. Members of the club can often offer good advice on where to shop for a scope.

In any event you should first look through the pages of magazines such as *Sky and Telescope, Popular Science,* or *Natural History* magazine for information and advertisements about telescopes. Use the Yellow Pages of your phone directory under telescopes to see the stores that are offering them for sale. Also write to some of the companies listed on page 82 for information and prices of their scopes.

Make your decision only after you have considered the

kinds and costs of the telescopes available. Make sure that a tripod is included or that you put aside enough money to buy one. Carefully read the instructions about setting up and operating the telescope. Try to have an older person who knows something about telescopes help you at first to set up and use the scope. In the next chapter, we'll tell you about some of the exciting things in the night sky that you can observe with a telescope.

CHAPTER 8

SOME SPECIAL SKY SIGHTS

Solar Eclipses

EVERYTHING that sunlight falls on casts a shadow. That includes you, a tree, a building, a mountain, the earth, and the moon. Sometimes that moon's shadow falls on the earth. This can happen only when the moon is in its new phase—when it is between the earth and the sun. When the lineup is straight and just right, the moon's shadow falls across the earth.

If you were in that shadow you would see the moon hide the sun. You would be seeing a solar eclipse. The moon casts two kinds of shadows. One is the very dark center shadow called an *umbra.* Around the small, dark umbra is a larger circle of shadow that is not as dark; it is called the *penumbra.*

When the umbra reaches the earth's surface, it is a circle of shadow about 50 to 150 miles across. Because of the earth's rotation, the umbra sweeps rapidly across the earth's surface. If you are in the path of the umbra, you would see the outline of the moon move across the face of the sun. For a few minutes the moon would just cover the sun, and you would see a total eclipse.

During the few minutes of totality, a strange and beautiful sight appears in the sky. The sunlight fades away and some of the brighter stars can be seen. At the moment that the moon completely hides the sun's disc, a halo of bright gases around the sun becomes visible. The sun's *corona* appears like a crown of fire around the central darkness of the moon's outline.

The moon's penumbra falls on a much larger area of the earth's surface. If you are in the path of the penumbra you see only a partial eclipse of the sun.

Never look directly at the sun during a solar eclipse. It may seem dark, but your eyes can be badly damaged by the sun's rays even in a few minutes. Even more dangerous is to look at the sun with binoculars or a telescope.

Here's how to look at a solar eclipse safely: Use a small telescope or a pair of binoculars and a sheet of white paper. Point the telescope or binoculars at the sun with the paper underneath the other end of the scope. Move

the paper up and down until the disc of the sun is in focus.
Look only at the paper. You will be able to see the movement of the moon across the face of the sun from beginning to end.

Even without telescope or binoculars you can view an
eclipse safely. Take a sheet of cardboard and punch a
round pinhole in it. The pinhole will allow the light of
the sun to come through. You can focus the light on the
sheet of white paper as directed in the paragraph above.

Each year there are one or two solar eclipses visible
some place on the earth. The problem for observers is
that these eclipses rarely occur at places you can easily
get to. For example, many total eclipses are visible only
over the oceans or on land areas far away from where
you live.

Between the date of publication of this book and the
end of the twentieth century there is only one total solar
eclipse visible in North America. It will occur on February 26, 1979. The umbra will travel from the Pacific
Ocean across the northwestern corner of the United
States.

There are many other total solar eclipses between now
and the end of the century. But you would have to go to
other continents to see them. For information about
where and when each of the year's eclipses is visible,
consult an almanac for the year or a magazine for astronomers such as *Sky and Telescope.*

Lunar Eclipses

Just as the earth sometimes passes through a shadow cast by the moon, the moon sometimes passes through a shadow cast by the earth. We call that a *lunar eclipse*. We can see the round shadow of the earth move across the face of the moon. When a lunar eclipse takes place, it can be seen all over the night side of the earth.

If the whole moon passes through the earth's shadow it is called a *total lunar eclipse*. But sometimes only part of the moon passes through the shadow. We call that a *partial lunar eclipse*. A lunar eclipse can take place only during the full moon phase.

You can view a lunar eclipse with your unaided eye or with binoculars or a telescope. There are usually one or more eclipses of the moon each year, each visible to half of the earth. You should be able to see at least one of them without any difficulty. Check an almanac, *Sky and Telescope* magazine, *Natural History* magazine, or a nearby museum or planetarium for information about the date and time.

Occultations

Occultations are kinds of eclipses. At times the moon or one of the planets may pass in front of a bright star. At other times the moon may pass in front of one of the planets. One of the planets may even pass in front of a more distant planet. The word "occultation" means a covering over or hiding.

While you can see an occultation with your unaided eye, a telescope or a pair of binoculars will give you a better view. To find out the dates and times of occultation for the year, consult an almanac or one of the sources listed above.

Auroras or Northern Lights

Sometimes the night sky is filled with shifting greenish or reddish lights. They may look like shimmering veil-like curtains. They may look like rays from searchlights in the sky. At times they may last all night long.

These lights are called *auroras*. In the Northern Hemisphere they are called the *aurora borealis* or northern lights. You can see them on many nights from the northern states and from Canada and Alaska.

Auroras are caused by electrical charges in the upper atmosphere that make the air glow. The electric charge comes from particles the sun sends out. Auroras can occur at any time but are more likely when the sun is very active and producing large numbers of sunspots.

Star Watching with a Telescope

On page 14 we spoke about the double stars Alcor and Mizar in the Big Dipper. These are the next to the last stars in the handle. Look at them through a telescope. You can easily separate Alcor and Mizar, but also you can see another star between them. It seems that Mizar is itself a double star.

There are many such double stars visible through even a small telescope. One of the most beautiful is a double star called *Albireo* in the constellation of the Swan. (See page 28.) One of the stars is orange while the other is bluish. The bright star Regulus in the constellation of the Lion is a double star. For further information about double stars consult one of the sources listed on page 83.

Still another interesting star sight through a telescope is the color of a star. Many stars when viewed with the unaided eye seem dim and white but through a telescope are seen as bright and colorful. Look at the star at the end of the bowl in the Big Dipper. It is called *Kochab*. It looks like just a dim star, but through a telescope it appears bright and orange in color. Read through chapters two and three to find some other stars that have colors.

The Orion Nebula

Look below the belt in the constellation of the Hunter (Orion) to the small group of stars hanging down that mark his sword. Look at the central star in the sword through a pair of binoculars or a small telescope. The star is surrounded by a pale cloud of glowing gas called a *nebula*.

A nebula is a huge cloud of gas in space. Some nebulas

The Lagoon Nebula in the constellation of the Archer (*Sagittarius*) glows with light because of the radiation of very hot stars in the center of the nebula.

are luminous and give off light because of nearby stars. You may be able to see five pinpoints of light in the Orion nebula. These make up the second star in the sword. Incidentally, the top star in the sword can be seen as a triple star through a telescope, while the bottom star in the sword is a double star. Check some of the sources on page 83 for information about other nebulas you can see with a telescope.

Star Clusters

Look at the star chart on page 34 to locate a small group of stars called the Seven Sisters of the Pleiades. Through an unaided eye it looks like six or seven rather dim stars close together. But look at it through a telescope. You'll see a host of dozens or even hundreds of stars.

This is an example of a star cluster, a large group of stars fairly close to each other in space. There are several different kinds of star clusters, such as an open cluster or a globular cluster. To find out more about them and where to look to observe them, you need an observing handbook such as one of those listed on page 83.

The Andromeda Galaxy

To find the Andromeda galaxy, start with the star in the northeast corner of the Great Square of the Winged Horse (see page 31). Go two stars farther to the northeast and then two stars north. You will see a faint patch of light in the night sky. Look at it through a telescope or binoculars.

You can see more than one million stars in this photo of two globular star clusters near the center of our Milky Way galaxy. *(facing page)*

The star cluster called the *Pleiades* is in the constellation of the Bull (*Taurus*). Surrounding the stars are shimmering veils made up of tiny particles of interstellar dust that shine by reflected light. *(below)*

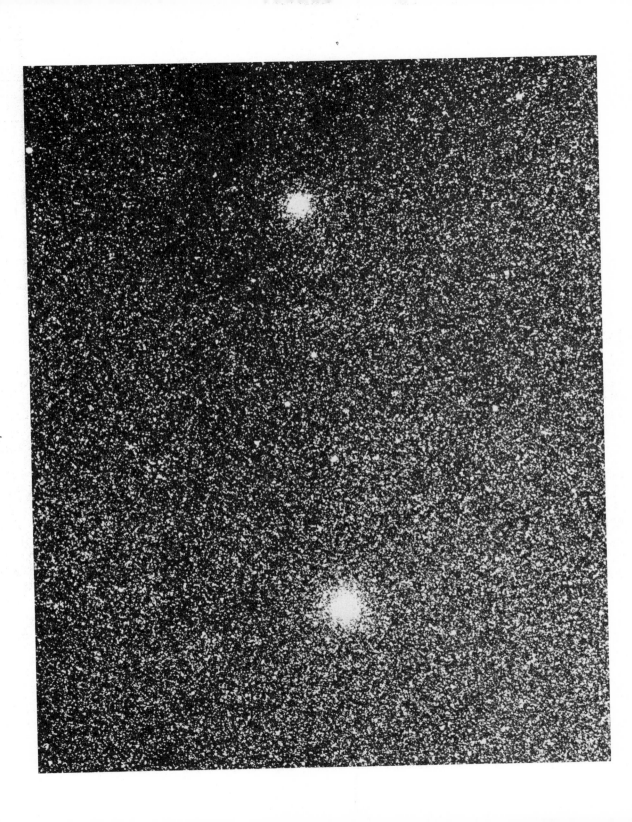

You are looking at the light coming from over 100 billion stars, part of a huge group of stars called a galaxy. The Andromeda galaxy is in the shape of a spiral, very much like that of our own galaxy, the Milky Way. It is so far away from us that even large telescopes cannot make out individual stars.

The few thousand stars that you can see with your unaided eye become hundreds of thousands and even millions with a telescope. Stars take on brilliant colors and planets show a disc. The moon becomes a real world out in space. Double stars, triple stars, nebulas, clusters, distant galaxies, all become more interesting when you actually see them in the night sky. As never before, you begin to realize that our planet earth is just a small speck in an enormous universe.

Astronomy is probably the oldest science in the world. As far back as there are records, we find mention of people looking at the stars and wondering about them. In 1609, the great Italian scientist Galileo first looked up at the night sky with a telescope. He saw and wrote about the moons of Jupiter, the craters of the moon, and the thousands of stars that make up the Milky Way.

You can see the Great Galaxy in the constellation of Andromeda even without a telescope. On a clear, dark night it appears as a faint, fuzzy patch of light. This enormous star system is one of the closest galaxies to our own Milky Way galaxy, yet it is more than two million light years distant.

The spiral arms in this galaxy (M33) in the constellation called *Triangulum* are clearly visible. The giant pinwheel probably contains billions upon billions of stars, as does our own galaxy.

Since the time of Galileo, astronomy and astronomical observing have become more and more advanced. Larger and better telescopes were built and housed in true observatories. Instruments such as the spectroscope, the radio telescope, and the space probe have all advanced our knowledge of the stars and the planets.

Today we are still exploring stars and the nature of the universe. Astronomers are studying and learning about how stars are born and how they die, about the size and shape of the universe, and about whether life exists anywhere else in our solar system or in our galaxy.

A study of the night sky can lead you to a lifetime hobby in astronomy. When you learn to recognize the stars and the constellations, you will always remember them, even in later years. And for those of you who are interested and continue your studies in college, the hobby of looking at the night sky may become, as it has for others, a career in astronomy.

Astrology and the Zodiac

What kind of person are you? Are you calm? Are you talkative? Are you friendly? Are you courageous? Astrologers believe that your character and fate are in the stars. You may not believe that (see page 22 for why astrology is not a science), but you might like to be an astrologer for fun.

Here's how. First you need to find your sign of the zodiac. Locate your birth date on the chart below and use it to find your sign.

Here is what astrologers would say about your sign: The "ruling planets" include eight planets (not the earth), the sun, and the moon. Find your sign and read your description. Does it sound like you? Ask a friend to listen to your description and tell you if he thinks it is accurate.

Capricorn December 22–January 19
Ruling planet: Saturn—planet of duty, responsibility, and discipline.
Characteristics: Practical, ambitious, cautious, restrained.

Aquarius January 20–February 18

Ruling planet: Uranus—planet of independence and impulsiveness.

Characteristics: Original, independent, natural, nonconforming.

Pisces February 19–March 20

Ruling planet: Neptune—planet of imagination and mystery.

Characteristics: Emotional, changeable, creative, irresolute.

Aries March 21– April 19

Ruling planet: Mars—planet of courage and energy.

Characteristics: Courageous, impulsive, aggressive, self-involved.

Taurus April 20–May 20

Ruling planet: Venus—planet of beauty, love, and peace.

Characteristics: Calm, practical, unexcitable, resolute.

Gemini May 21–June 20

Ruling planet: Mercury—planet of speed and intelligence.

Characteristics: Restless, talkative, changeable.

Cancer June 21–July 22
Ruling planet: The moon—emotions and feelings.
Characteristics: Moody, possessive, determined.

Leo July 23–August 22
Ruling planet: The sun—drive and self-will.
Characteristics: Leadership, generosity, self-importance.

Virgo August 23–September 22
Ruling planet: Mercury—planet of speed and intelligence.
Characteristics: Choosy, active, intellectual.

Libra September 23–October 22
Ruling planet: Venus—planet of beauty, love and peace.
Characteristics: Fair-minded, peace-loving.

Scorpio October 23–November 21
Ruling planet: Pluto—planet of power and strength.
Characteristics: Determined, devious, possessive.

Sagittarius November 22–December 21
Ruling planet: Jupiter—planet of kindness and generosity.
Characteristics: Friendly, enthusiastic, optimistic.

Telescope Sources

Cave Optical Company (Reflectors)
4137 East Anaheim Street
Long Beach, California 90804

Celestron International (Catadioptrics)
2835 Columbia Street
Torrance, California 90503

Colonial Optical Company, Inc. (Refractors)
8401 S. LaCienega Boulevard
Englewood, California 90301

Criterion Manufacturing Company (Reflectors, Catadioptrics)
620 Oakwood Avenue
West Hartford, Connecticut 06110

Edmund Scientific Company (Refractors, Reflectors)
300 Edscorp Building
Barrington, New Jersey 08007

Optical Craftsmen, Inc. (Reflectors)
20962 Itasca Street
Chatsworth, California 91311

Questar Corporation (Catadioptrics)
New Hope, Pennsylvania 18938

Star-Liner Company (Reflectors)
1106 South Columbus Boulevard
Tucson, Arizona 85711

Swift Instrument Corporation (Refractors)
P.O. Box 562
San Jose, California 95106

Tasco Sales, Inc. (Refractors)
P.O. Box 380878
Miami, Florida 33138

Unitron Instruments, Inc. (Refractors)
101 Crossways Park West
Woodbury, New York 11797

FOR FURTHER READING
AND RESEARCH

Asimov, Isaac. *How Did We Find Out about Comets?* New York: Walker, 1975.

Branley, Franklyn M. *Comets, Meteoroids, and Asteroids.* New York: Crowell, 1974.

————. *The Nine Planets.* New York: Crowell, 1971.

Dietz, David. *Stars and the Universe.* New York: Random House, 1968.

Gallant, Roy A. *Exploring the Planets.* New York: Doubleday, 1967.

————. *Exploring the Universe.* New York: Doubleday, 1968.

Heuer, Kenneth. *City of the Stargazers.* New York: Scribner's, 1972.

Ley, Willy. *Gas Giants: The Largest Planets.* New York: McGraw-Hill, 1969.

Moore, Patrick. *The Picture History of Astronomy.* New York: Grosset & Dunlap, 1967.

Paul, Henry E. *Outer Space Photography for the Amateur.* Philadelphia: Chilton, 1967.

PERIODICALS

Sky and Telescope (monthly)
49–50–51 Bay State Road
Cambridge, Mass. 02138

The Observer's Handbook (yearly edition)
The Royal Astronomical Society of Canada
124 Merton Street
Toronto M4S 2Z2, Canada

INDEX